I0521178

Storylandia

The Wapshott Journal
of Fiction

Issue 24

The Wapshott Press

Storylandia, Issue 24, The Wapshott Journal of Fiction, ISSN 1947-5349, ISBN 978-1-942007-16-6 is published at intervals by the Wapshott Press, now a 501(c)(3) nonprofit, PO Box 31513, Los Angeles, California, 90031-0513, telephone 323-201-7147. All correspondence can be sent to The Wapshott Press, PO Box 31513, LA CA 90031-0513. Visit our website at www.WapshottPress.org to learn more. This work is copyright © 2018 by Storylandia. The Wapshott Journal of Fiction, Los Angeles, California. Copyright © 2018 James White and is reprinted here with the copyright owner's permission.

Storylandia is always seeking quality original short stories, novelettes, and novellas. Please have a look at our submission guidelines at www.Storylandia.WapshottPress.org or email the editor at editor@wapshottpress.org

The Wapshott Press wishes to express our deepest gratitude to Laura Matulac for the proofread, editorial support, and the lovely cover artwork. Also thanks to Emmett Matulac for his invaluable help and enthusiasm at all times.

Cover: "Chassy" by Laura Matulac

Storylandia

The Wapshott Journal of Fiction

Founded in 2009

Issue 24, Winter 2018

Edited by Ginger Mayerson

Chassy

By James White

Chassy

By James White

1

"My Lord, they're too close!" A lady stood by herself at the stern of the SS Normandie looking at the ocean liner's wake. The breeze coming off the Hudson River ruffled her long dark skirt and carried her anxious admonition across the promenade deck. A strand of blonde hair escaped her scarlet beret and waved against her cheek.

Bridge Appleton, twelve years old, looked up from his book and stared at the lady's silhouette, framed by the receding New York skyline as the Normandie made its way down the river toward Rockaway Point.

People strolled by his deck chair muttering about what the lady was up to. "Man overboard? A collision? Come on, let's take a look."

The lady ignored the curious crowd and kept her position looking neither left nor right, but straight ahead at an incident taking place beyond Bridge's warm blanket and comfortable chair.

The breeze increased into a wind

"Nutcase," Bridge said. He turned his face away from the wind and went back to reading Dashiell Hammett's exciting new whodunit mystery, *The Maltese Falcon*.

A steward walked by carrying a brass gong, suspended on a string, and a small mallet. He was immaculately dressed in a black sailor hat, starched whites, and gleaming patent leather shoes. "Bong, bong," the gong's sonorous tone echoed across the deck as the steward tapped it with his mallet.

"First seating for dinner in ten minutes," he announced.

The crowd of onlookers surrounding the lady turned away from the railing. "A whole bunch of nothin'," somebody commented as the people headed toward the dining room.

"Who cares?" somebody else said. "Stupid sail-boats is all it is."

Once the deck was clear, Bridge put his book down again and pulled off his lap blanket. The lady was still looking over the railing.

"My gracious," he heard her say. "Why on earth are they doing that?"

Bridge got up from his chair. It must be something.

Bridge was traveling to Marseille with his parents. It was supposed to be a family vacation, but he was already bored and he dreaded the weeks of captivity that stretched ahead. While they celebrated their departure with dancing and champagne, he entertained himself out on deck with his book.

He glanced up and down the deck as he stepped toward the lady. The coast was clear. I'll sneak a look on my way in to dinner.

Sailboats, two of them, darted in and out of the Normandie's wake. The late afternoon sun lit up their sails and turned their spray into flying diamonds as the boats churned through the rough water in Jamaica Bay.

The lady glanced at Bridge and pointed at the sailboats, one in front of the other, racing along the Normandie's right side. The pitch of the liner's engines picked up a notch and Bridge felt the ship shudder, then surge ahead, but the sailboats doggedly kept up.

"They must be having a heck of a time of it out

there," she said.

"It looks dangerous," Bridge replied.

Some of the sailboats' crew were pulling on ropes while the two captains, each standing at their boat's wheel, shouted orders through a megaphone. Other crew members leaned out over the water on the high side using their weight to keep their boat from capsizing.

"I don't know how much longer they can keep up," the lady said. She pulled her shawl tight around her shoulders.

Bridge nodded. He couldn't turn away.

The trailing sailboat caught Bridge's attention. A big sail had broken free of its restraining ropes. People were trying to capture the flapping canvas as the boat lurched to one side and pitched into the relentless waves.

"Oh my Lord, they're in trouble!" The lady gasped.

Bridge cupped his hands around his mouth and shouted a warning, but it was hopeless.

The leading boat sailed on, its crew, concentrating on their own challenges, were oblivious to their partner's distress.

Just when it seemed like the disabled boat's crew had regained control, a gust of wind tore the loose sail out of the crew's hands and the long boom whipped across the deck, scattering crew members in all directions.

Two splashes appeared alongside the boat, but Bridge couldn't make out who or what was in the water.

The boat fell behind the Normandie. It was getting hard to see, but Bridge and the lady both shouted when a wave washed across the boat and turned it on its side. Slowly, like a falling tree, the tall mast fell until only the boat's keel showed above the water.

"Those poor people," the lady said. "They're goners."

"We gotta do something," Bridge looked from side to side. He and the lady were alone. The Normandie's deck lights came on in the evening gloom. The tinkling of piano music came from inside.

"I'm gonna tell the captain." Bridge turned away from the rail and ran into somebody.

"Bridge! There you are!" A hand clamped on Bridge's shoulder. "We've been looking all over for you. You've missed dinner and you're not even dressed. Mother is beside herself!" Bridge's father wore a formal dark suit and bow tie. A scarf hung loose around his neck. He flipped his cigarette overboard.

"Dad! Dad!" Bridge hopped up and down, eyes wide. He pointed in the direction of the accident which was now hidden in shadows. "There's been an accident. We gotta turn around. They need help."

Bridge's father looked into the darkness and shook his head.

"Poor fellows. A bit of bad luck, I'll say. Not much we can do about it, Sport. Surely somebody on the shore will help them."

The lady coughed.

"But Dad! Can't we drop them a lifeboat or something? I'm going to tell the captain." Bridge twisted and tried to escape, but he couldn't break his father's grasp.

The air turned cold as the Normandie made a gentle left turn and nosed into the Atlantic. The ocean breeze buffeted them with salty gusts. In the distance behind them, specks of light appeared, but it was impossible to tell from where they came.

His father's face glowed from the deck lights.

"Sorry, Sport, but the captain's not going to turn around. We're still in a narrow ship channel. He would never change course this close to shore with no navigation lights to guide us. It could be catastrophic." He lit another cigarette, took a deep breath, and exhaled into the darkness. "I'm afraid those boys will have to fend for themselves."

Bridge looked for the lady, but she had disappeared.

"You've missed your dinner and your Mother is−"

Bridge started to cry. "But people might be dying," he sobbed.

Bridge's father led him away from the railing. "Buck up, son," he said in a low tone. "The sea is a risky place in a small boat. They're prepared for that, I'm sure." He ushered Bridge along the promenade deck. "Sometimes King Neptune demands tribute."

Bridge blew his nose on his sleeve. "But Dad! It's not funny! Those people..."

They went through a door into an empty companionway.

"That will be enough." Bridge's father shook his shoulder. "Go to the cabin and get dressed. Your Mother put out your dinner jacket and tie on your bunk. Maybe our steward can find something for you to eat. Hurry up. Mustn't keep her waiting any longer."

His father cleared his throat. "And let's not speak about this at the table, right Sport? You'll only distress her."

Bridge turned away and said nothing.

"Too dangerous," his mother told Bridge when he asked his parents for a sailboat on his fifteenth birthday.

His father dropped his newspaper and raised an eyebrow when he heard Bridge's request.

"People fall off those little traps and drown every day," his mother said.

She was right, of course. The image of that boat lying in the water behind the Normandie, looking more like a piece of driftwood than a sailboat, had disturbed him ever since that night, but it also fascinated him. Night after night, as he fell asleep he relived that horrible moment. *How could something so beautiful and exciting turn into disaster so fast?*

Bridge took his father's advice when he started at Hollywood High School and he joined the gymnastics team. He worked hard at his studies, and on the side horse and the parallel bars, but still the dread and fascination of sailboats haunted him. So he read Melville and Conrad and Joshua Slocum and he fulfilled his tormented dreams of sailing by becoming a knowledgeable bystander.

Later, in college, Bridge would drive to Long Beach, stand at the end of the Long Beach breakwater and revisit that night on the Normandie. With the spray in his face, he would wave to the bigger boats that ventured out of the harbor. The boats looked beautiful, rushing through a magical space between wind and waves, but for Bridge the beauty was only part of the spectacle. He knew as well that they were a hair-breadth away from disaster and certain death.

It was the start of the sailing season, April 1936, when Deborah Cunningham invited her boyfriend Bridge and their friends Patsy and Charles to dinner at The Wharf, one of Bridge's favorite watering holes that offered fresh seafood with views of the harbor.

Below them, outside, men scurried like ants

around the cargo ships and steamers that lined the long warehouse docks. Inside, the sound of crystal and china clinked amid soft piano jazz and the low murmurs of attentive waiters.

"It's sailing season again, God help us." Deborah gave Bridge a sidelong glance. "Another four months of sitting on rocks and freezing to death watching sailboats dart in and out of the fog."

Bridge and Deborah made a striking couple when they were out together; she preferred to wear unpopular styles and always looked good in them. She tucked her wavy blonde hair inside berets of all colors, wrapped herself in capes and shawls and wore boots. He often sported a jaunty captain's cap and blazer and he would never be seen on the town without wearing white linen trousers and a flashy bow tie.

Bridge smiled. "Sometimes they capsize. Then the drama picks up."

"That just makes me feel colder."

"Why don't you try tennis?" Patsy suggested. "It's all the rage, you know. City College just built some clay courts next to the football field. I think Chassy and I are good for a rousing set of mixed doubles. Aren't we, Chassy dear?" She patted Charles' hand to get his attention.

Charles sighed and lit a cigarette. "How about I ask the waiter to mix us a drink instead?" Tennis was not his sport.

A petite redhead with a temper and a sunny smile, Patsy had worked her way out of her parents' tarpaper shack, hidden behind orange groves, and into the glamorous thoroughfares of Los Angeles using her wits and natural charm.

Charles, a tall, lanky southern boy who came west with his brother riding the rails, had become friends with Bridge while competing together in Hollywood High's gymnastics team.

The four young people became close when fate tossed them together at Los Angeles City College. They built a friendship while managing sporting event ticket and souvenir sales every weekend in the school's cramped ticket booth.

"What about horseback riding?" Deborah contributed to the tease. "There's a riding stables near Griffith Park–"

"Oh, I'd love to go horseback riding," Patsy squealed. "My grandmother sent me this most beautiful pair of jodhpurs. Before Grandpa lost everything in the stock market crash, Grams competed in the state invitationals and was always a finalist. I've been dying to use 'em just so I could tell her."

Deborah gave Patsy a pat on the arm. "She would be so proud."

"No kidding, Deborah." Patsy flashed a look. "Don't patronize me. I mean it. She was one of the best."

"Please, ladies," Bridge interrupted before Deborah could retort back. "Wild horses won't deter me from my perch on the breakwater."

Deborah glanced at Patsy and rolled her eyes. The ladies silently made up and resigned themselves to another of Bridge's rants.

"...and if you're lucky," Bridge paused and looked around the table, "one of these days, I might just show you first-hand what sailing is all about."

Deborah plunged her knife and fork into her abalone steak as if it was about to make a break for it. "Don't bother. Second hand is plenty enough for me."

After a final round of cocktails and a walk around the wharf, Deborah snuggled up against

Bridge and whispered, "Cicada Club?"

The Club was originally an elegant haberdashery on South Olive Street where Deborah's mother often shopped for the most sophisticated styles in chiffon, satin, charmeuse, and organdy, accented with fine-worked lace, beads, and sequin.

Deborah's parents loved the shop's intricately painted Spanish-beamed ceiling and hand-carved oak paneling. When it came up for sale, they saved it from the wrecking ball and financed its conversion to a nightclub. Now, Deborah managed the bar when she wasn't on the customer side with Bridge.

Bridge straightened his tie then squeezed Deborah's hand. His brave proposition in front of witnesses needed a follow-up. "Don't be surprised if I take you sailing someday."

Deborah got behind the wheel of her Packard Eight and started up while Charles and Patsy climbed into the back seat. Bridge barely had time to get in before his girlfriend floored it. "Keep talkin', sailor."

One day, when the fog hung back along the horizon and the harbor was crowded with boats of all types, Bridge overheard two fellows on the Long Beach pier talk about selling a sailboat.

Bridge was on his way to the breakwater when he stopped in his tracks. A grizzled fellow with long greasy hair tied in a ponytail and smoking a blackened meerschaum pipe was doing the talking. His partner, another shipwrecked derelict, nodded with a wry smile under his wool watch cap.

"Did I hear you say you want to sell a boat?" Bridge interrupted the two while they grumbled over a tub of water filled with dead fish and beer bottles. Two fishing poles jutted out from the pier's railing.

"That's right," came the reply. The men resumed their conversation. They never looked up.

The water beneath the pier glistened in the warm noon-day sun. Seagulls squawked, a candy vendor walked by ringing a chain of small bells. Bridge leaned in close to the men. "Can I see it?"

Bridge's vision of the Normandie incident, and his anxieties that sailed along with it, disappeared over a far horizon.

Ponytail sighed, looked up and blew smoke in Bridge's face. "Hundred dollars gets you the boat, main and foresails, rigging, and an anchor all in fair condition. Ready to sail. You interested?"

Bridge's eyes watered in the acrid cloud. He felt his heart race. He hesitated for an instant and then recklessly plunged ahead. Here's my chance. A transaction done in secret. Mother will never know.

"I might be."

"It's tied up at the end of C dock. Gate's locked, though. I'll have to take you. You sure you're interested? I don't want to make the trip fer nothin'."

Ponytail squinted at Bridge with his one good eye and snarled.

Bridge took a deep breath and felt the relief of having made a decision. "If I like it I'll buy it. My name is Bridge. Bridge Appleton."

The crusty character smiled a contemptuous smile and winked at his castaway companion. "Call me Ross."

Bridge felt Ross' calloused, leathery skin scrape against his hand while they shook. It felt like a sailor's hand.

Ross and Bridge stood at the end of C dock and stared down at a weathered, neglected sailboat.

"There she is. You can see the rigging is good

and secure," Ross said, pointing at the boat's rusty metal fittings and bleached woodwork. "Tiller's mountings could be tightened up a bit, but that's minor. She could use a coat of paint. It's been a coupla' years. Do ya want 'a check her down below?"

"No thanks, I can see all I need from here." Bridge was too embarrassed to ask dumb questions in front of a real sailor. Instead, he stared at something that wasn't there. It was liable to sink at any minute, but Bridge saw adventure. Forbidden adventure he'd only watched from afar.

After ten long minutes, Ross spit and headed back to the gate. "Damned lubber," Ross said loud enough for Bridge to hear. "Another waste of an afternoon."

Ross's words made Bridge look up from his floating daydream. He saw Ross walking away and panicked. "Will you take a check?"

"Your boyfriend has purchased a sailboat," Bridge announced that night when he met Deborah at the Club to celebrate their fifth anniversary going together. He handed her a hat box. "And I hereby commission you first mate along with all the privileges that befit the position."

Deborah cringed as she opened the box. "You didn't."

She stared at a white sailor's hat with an anchor stitched in the front.

"I most certainly did." Bridge beamed. "She's a beaut, and I'm thinking what a wonderful time we'll have sailing over the ocean blue together. You and me. We'll take in all the exotic ports of call, Istanbul, Zanzibar, Rio de Janeiro."

He set the hat on Deborah's head. "Great hat,

huh? I know you like hats. Let's see how it looks..."

Deborah grabbed the hat out of his hands and dropped it on the bar. "My dear, sweet lunatic. I get seasick standing on a pier. I wouldn't last a minute on your bouncy old boat. The very idea makes my stomach turn."

"Once your stomach's empty you'll feel better." Bridge lowered his eyes and fingered the hat's brim.

Deborah shook her head and balled her fists. "You wouldn't like the looks of me puking over the side."

Bridge shuddered. "Deborah, please." He let go of the hat and grabbed his drink.

"No. And that's final."

"Now, be a good sport on our anniversary." The condensation from Bridge's drink that had collected on the polished oak bar stained the bottom rim of the hat.

"Have you ever been seasick?" Deborah hopped off her bar stool. "I'll have you know I have endured endless hours in the company of happy, chatty people eating and drinking while I clung to a railing, my hair sticky with vomit, and prayed for death. It's not a pretty sight."

She grabbed her purse from under the bar and walked toward the coat check. "Keep your damn hat."

2

Bridge parked his Packard One-Twenty coupe at the C dock gate and sat for a moment. He rallied his courage while his car cooled and quieted. He had put off visiting the boat for a week since he bought it for two very good reasons: he was worried about what he had done and he was afraid his mother might find out.

The physical act of unlocking the gate and

driving across the dock's heavy planks built up his confidence. The planks creaked and sagged under the weight of his car as he slowly made his way to the end of the dock. Other sailboats, tied up on either side of the dock, bobbed in the gentle swell, their rigging clanged against tall masts.

"Thar she blows," Bridge whispered when his boat came in sight. His heart raced and he felt dizzy as the enormity of what he had done manifested into the boat sitting in front of him.

After setting the handbrake, Bridge took his time getting out of the car, breathing in the salt air to calm his nerves.

He pulled out a chair from the car trunk and found a spot that gave him an unobstructed view. It was a warm, sunny day and he sat with the sun high over his shoulder, illuminating the boat's deck and rigging. He studied the three mooring ropes that secured the boat to the dock. Their constant movement, alternating from slack to taut, captivated him, but he didn't see the long tentacles of seaweed that dangled from each rope into the water.

Alone on the quiet dock, with a thermos of rum befitting the occasion, the sun, sea air, and booze soothed him into a languid stupor. The peaceful setting displaced memories of shipwreck and disaster. Instead, he dreamed of lying with Deborah in his boat's cabin while on their maiden voyage to Catalina Island. They were sunburned and salty. He licked her bare shoulder and felt her shudder under his touch. Outside, porpoises leapt alongside and schools of flying fish flashed their silvery wings.

"Oh, Bridge," Deborah murmured, "I've never been so happy in all my life."

A flock of squawking seagulls woke Bridge

from his floating fantasy. Still groggy, he said good-bye to his boat, packed his chair and, empty thermos under his arm, went home.

A week later, Bridge brought his friends, Charles and Patsy, to show off.

It was a damp, chilly morning when the three of them made their way along C dock. A foghorn blasted earnestly behind the cold mists that covered the harbor. Other sounds; bells, whistles, and engine noises, took on an eerie, muffled quality, coming seemingly from out of nowhere.

Patsy held her coat tight around her and shivered. With her free hand, she clutched Charles' arm. "Deborah told me he doesn't know the first thing about sailing, despite what he says," she said in Charles' ear. She gave Bridge a quick glance, hoping he wasn't listening.

"Don't believe everything you hear," Bridge replied.

When they got to the end of the dock, Bridge stopped and pointed. "Ain't she a beaut! I bought it from an experienced seaman I met at the Long Beach pier. He hated to let it go and he assured me the boat was safe and fast! I saw a tear in his eye when I handed him the check."

Patsy took a deep breath and pulled on Charles' sleeve. "Promise me you won't do anything dangerous."

"Maybe he was crying for joy in anticipation of his next bottle," Charles suggested while he peered down and tried to make sense out of all the ropes and junk that littered the boat's deck.

The boat's mooring lines strained against the wind and tide.

"About 20 feet long, wouldn't you say?" Charles suggested.

"Big enough for all of us," Bridge exclaimed.

Patsy shook her head. "Maybe with a shoehorn."

The teak deck railings and tiller were bleached white and hung loose in their fittings. The few pieces of brass hardware were green with salt corrosion. The hull planking was cracked in places and badly in need of caulk and fresh paint. Below the waterline, a thick coat of algae covered the boat's bottom.

Bridge pointed to the passageway. "That's where Deborah and I'll live during long voyages."

Patsy looked at Charles and raised her eyebrows. "Do you think Deborah's wardrobe will fit in there?"

"I'll name her after the first person who falls overboard," Bridge announced with a false air of bravado. He put his hands on the slimy gunwale and felt the boat respond to his touch. The fear of leaving the safety of the dock and crossing over the watery gap into the boat consumed him. His romantic boating dreams vanished and visions of the boat foundering in the Normandie's wake came back. He had to clasp his knees tight to keep from embarrassing himself.

Don't stop now. He tried to hide a gasp as he put one foot into the cockpit. The boat tipped under his weight, catching him by surprise. All the watching and studying he'd done from the breakwater hadn't prepared him for his first step aboard. He ducked as the boom swung toward his head, then he lunged for the cabin rail to keep from falling backwards. Embarrassed, he turned his head and grinned back at Charles and Patsy. "She's as skittish as a thoroughbred."

Being onboard was an accomplishment and

Bridge felt his confidence return. The boat's rocking turned into a comforting feel, like a cradle.

"There are storage lockers in here," he shouted while sticking his head through the hatch and peering in the cabin.

Loose ropes and hardware swung about the deck and banged against the sides of the cabin as Bridge jostled into the tight space. "They're filled with empty liquor bottles, also some used tobacco products, and adult magazines. A couple of oars too. They might come in handy."

Bridge stuck his head back out the cabin passageway and gave his friends a smile of accomplishment. "It's cozy in here!"

"I'm cold," Patsy said.

"Well, don't just stand there," Bridge shouted back. "Climb aboard!"

"You go," Patsy said, looking at Charles. "I'm not getting close to that thing until it's completely scrubbed clean. It's filthy and smells like mold. You can play sailor if you want. I'm supposed to pick up Deborah in an hour. We'll bring back cleaning supplies."

"And some lunch," Charles added.

"Wait a minute." Bridge scrambled out of the cabin. "Give this to Patsy." He tossed Charles his key to the C dock gate. "Bring back a bottle of champagne, you never know when an occasion might arise."

After Patsy left, Charles climbed into the boat and ducked as the boom swung again. It smacked Bridge on the back of his head while he waved good-bye to Patsy.

"I feel like I'm in a Keystone Kops movie," Charles shouted, his voice high with excitement.

"Sit down, you big ape!" Bridge shouted back.

He held the back of his head with both hands and groaned. When the pain became bearable, he went back below deck and gathered up the girlie magazines and empty bottles.

Charles sat in a patch of green mold that covered the cockpit seats and felt his stomach give a lurch.

Bridge tossed an arm-full of trash over the side. "You get topside and sort out those sails," he said when he saw Charles' contorted face. "I'll untie these ropes and we'll take her for a test drive."

"Are you sure we're ready to go?" Charles crawled and scooted his way across the roof of the cabin to the bundle of canvas. "I don't know what I'm supposed to do." Water seeped into the seat of his pants.

"We're never gonna know if we don't learn," Bridge answered back, raising his voice to cover his uncertainty. "We'll just see how it feels and sail right back."

The fog was lifting, but the harbor appeared gloomy in the filtered sun. Bridge caught a glimpse of the breakwater's line of jagged gray rocks far off on the other side of the harbor. Spray, blown up from waves on the ocean side of the harbor, cascaded over the top of the rocks. The sight reminded him of the overturned sailboat that sank behind the Normandie.

With a brave huzzah, Bridge stifled his panic and untied the last dock line.

Charles added an excited whoop, exhilarated by the feeling of floating free.

Bridge grabbed the tiller and swung the long wooden handle from side to side. It wobbled loose in its mounting, but the rudder responded, churning up eddies behind the boat.

"Hoist the sail," Bridge commanded as the boat drifted away from the dock, pulled along by an ebb tide.

Charles clung to the mast with one hand and grabbed the bundle of canvas and ropes with the other. "How do you do that?" he said as the gap between them and the dock increased until they were beyond hope.

The canvas was encrusted with guano, wet from the fog. Charles rubbed his hand, sticky with guano, on his trousers.

"It's simple," Bridge shouted. "I've watched it done a hundred times. Find the rope that goes up to the top of the mast. Tie one end of the rope to the sail's top end, and tie the other two ends of the sail to the mast and the end of the boom. Then pull on the other end of the rope."

"Look at me," he beamed, sitting at the helm and trying to look confident. "I'm steering."

The boat drifted sideways into the harbor and toward the channel that led out to sea.

Charles grabbed a rope that dangled in front of him. "What's a boom?" He turned to face Bridge. "Maybe you should steer us back around?"

"No, dammit," Bridge yelled back. "Get busy hoisting that sail."

Charles looked at the top of the mast and gulped while watching it sway to and fro. "Maybe this is it!" he shouted when he saw the rope in his hand led to the top.

The boat was gone when Patsy and Deborah got back to C dock with lunch and cleaning supplies.

"That's funny," Patsy said as they looked around the empty marina. "I'm positive this is where we were."

Deborah saw a small boat bobbing in the misty distance. It was moving in the direction of the breakwater. Somebody was standing next to the mast and wrestling with a pile of canvas.

"Could that be them?" Deborah pointed in the direction of the boat.

"By gosh, I think it is," Patsy replied. She pointed at the boat "I told him not to do anything dangerous."

Deborah sighed. "I think we're too late."

Charles tied the rope as best he could to a grommet he found in the pile of canvas. Forgetting the rest of Bridge's instructions, and too intimidated to ask again, he clutched the other end of the rope and pulled. To his utter amazement, the bundle of canvas traveled up the mast.

"I'm doing it," he exclaimed. "I'm raising the sail!"

"And not a moment too soon," Bridge roared back.

Pulling with enthusiasm, Charles hauled a corner of the sail up as far as it would go. The other two ends billowed against the mast and wrapped around the rigging. A small part worked itself free and fluttered proudly in the wind.

"That doesn't look right," Bridge said. "Are you sure you got the sail attached properly?"

Deborah pointed at a patch of gray canvas flapping in the breeze.

"I wonder why they're flying a flag?" she said. "Shouldn't there be a sail? It is a sailboat, isn't it?"

Patsy nodded. "Maybe it's a distress flag, you

think? Maybe we should call the cops, or the Navy or something."

Charles tried to free the canvas from the rigging lines, but it was wrapped tight. "I can't get 'holt of it," he shouted. "Got any other ideas?"

Bridge watched the line of big rocks loom closer. He gripped the tiller with both hands until his knuckles turned white. A feeling of helplessness set in and the vision of that boat bobbing on its side behind the Normandie left him paralyzed.

"Hold on!" He clenched his teeth and stared at the churning water around him. King Neptune appeared below the surface and shook his trident at Bridge in triumph.

"Ahoy there!" Charles shouted. A large motorboat approached them from another part of the harbor at high speed, its twin diesel engines emitting a powerful, rumbling sound. He waved as it drew closer and slowed down.

"Could you use a hand there?" A voice came across the water.

Bridge answered back with as much aplomb as he could muster. "Why yes. Hope you don't mind. That would be splendid."

The motorboat's massive bow and superstructure cast a long shadow over the rescue scene. Sounds of laughter and kitchen noises came through one of the portholes. A heavy rope dropped from the boat's stern and landed at Charles' feet.

"Tie the line to your bow cleat and I'll tow you," a man, standing at the back of the motorboat, shouted at Charles.

"What's a bow cleat?" Charles yelled back.

The man shook his head and a loud laugh came

from the motorboat's pilot house.

"The pointy end of the boat, young man," came the reply. "Never mind the cleat, just tie it anywhere close to the pointy end, good and tight. Hurry now, you're running out of room."

Charles wrapped the line around the base of the forestay and secured it with as many knots as he could dream up.

"Hold on!" came the voice from the motorboat's pilot house. The line snapped out of the water and drew taut as the motorboat roared to life.

Charles hugged the mast with both arms and as they twisted around and moved away from the breakwater. A scraping noise came from below the water as the little boat's keel dragged across a submerged rock.

"Where do you want me to take you?" Came a voice from the motorboat.

"Over there," Charles shouted, pointing toward their girlfriends.

Deborah and Patsy stood on the dock waving frantically.

"Looks like a good destination to me," came the reply.

When they reached C dock, a tall man wearing a knitted cap and pea coat stepped out from the motorboat's wheelhouse while Charles untied all of his knots and freed the boat from its tether.

The man had a commanding presence.

"You boys could use a lesson or two. I wouldn't take the girls for a ride just yet."

Patsy and Deborah stared at the man, open-mouthed, and tittered.

"He looks familiar," Patsy said. "Doesn't he look handsome?"

"I know. And famous, maybe."

"It's not Errol Flynn, that's for sure. And Clark Gable's too old. Robert Taylor maybe?"

"Thanks for the advice," Charles yelled. He waved as the man saluted and went into the pilot house.

Another man, standing at the controls, laughed and spun the boat's wheel.

The twin diesel engines roared again and the boat turned. It created a turbulent, rolling wake as it picked up speed and headed toward the harbor entrance in a cloud of exhaust.

The name displayed on the boat's transom was 'Missy.'

Charles let go of the mast. He stood boldly, balancing on the top of the cabin and raised a hand in salute. "Bridge," he yelled. "I think after a few more tries we might get the hang of this thing."

The motorboat's wake caused the sailboat to pitch wildly, catching Charles by surprise and knocking him off his feet. He tried to grab something, but nothing came his way.

Bridge cringed helplessly as Charles toppled forward. 'For the love of God, is this floating disaster ever going to end?' he wondered.

Charles twisted, trying to check his fall, but he landed with a splash on his back between the boat and the dock.

Patsy screamed.

The unexpected fall and the sudden, numbing cold made Charles gasp involuntarily. He took in a breath of water as he went under. Shock, and the onset of hypothermia, rendered him helpless. All he could do was watch the dappling sunlight dance across the surface above him as cold water filled his lungs.

Patsy looked at Deborah with terror in her

eyes. She stood frozen, unable to move.

"We have to do something." Deborah gulped and ran to the end of the dock. She lay down flat atop the wet, moldy planks and stretched her arm out as far as she could, but she couldn't reach him. The tide was pulling Charles away. "Grab him Bridge," she screamed.

"My boat's got a name," Bridge said as he leaned over the gunwale.

Charles' head knocked against the boat's rudder.

Bridge grabbed Charles by the shirt collar and pulled his head out of the water. "Where do ya think you're goin'?"

Charles didn't respond.

Bridge struggled to pull him in the boat, but try as he might, Charles was too heavy. Exhausted, Bridge just managed to keep Charles' head out of the water.

The faces of the drowned men that were left behind the Normandie appeared below the water's surface. "Don't leave us," they said.

"Go away," Bridge mumbled. He shuddered and turned away.

Charles began coughing and choking. He took a ragged breath and looked up at Bridge, wide-eyed, in shock.

"Fer Christ's sake, Bridge. Pull him out of the water!" Both girls were shouting.

"C'mon Charles, help me out here. On the count of three, heave ho." Bridge grabbed Charles under his arms and pulled with all his might. The boat leaned precariously over as Bridge tackled the dead weight.

Finally, Charles slid into the boat like a hooked

sea bass.

Too exhausted to move, Bridge knelt next to him, gasping for breath.

Charles curled up in a fetal position, shivering and coughing.

It was getting dark. The afternoon had never completely cleared up. The fog rolled back in and the temperature dropped.

"Chassy!" Patsy shouted. "You okay?"

Bridge gathered enough strength to reply. "Fetch the blanket from the trunk of the car. Sure wish we had some brandy."

Patsy returned with the blanket and tossed it with all her strength, but it landed in the water as the boat drifted away from the dock.

"The boat's moving again, Bridge!"

Bridge grabbed a handful of wet, mildewed rope. He held one end and threw the rest of it at Deborah. "Hold on to your end," he said.

Deborah recoiled as she looped the slimy rope around her wrists and tried to hold on as the slack played out through her fingers, following the drifting boat.

Bridge gathered his end until the line held taut and the boat stopped drifting.

"Good girl!" Bridge shouted hoarsely.

Deborah glared back at Bridge and kept hold of the rope. She forced herself not to look at her hands.

Charles raised his head. His chest heaved and he vomited seawater across the bottom of the boat. His tormented retching ended with an agonizing moan as he fell back on his side.

"For the love of God, Bridge," Patsy bawled. "Don't let him die."

Bridge looked at Patsy's distraught face and

nodded.

He gave the rope a determined yank and the sudden movement caused it to slip through Deborah's hands. Green slime collected in between her fingers.

"It's slipping!" Patsy watched in horror.

"What the hell?" Deborah grunted. She wrapped the rope in the hem of her dress and held on. Her exposed pink thighs gleamed in what was left of the afternoon's sunlight.

Bridge hauled on the rope hand over hand until he was able to grab the edge of the dock. With all the strength left in him, he pulled the boat up alongside. A fingernail gave way as he clutched at the weathered, splintered wood. For a moment, the boat sat suspended between the dock and the sea, held in place by a single, fragile line. Nobody moved.

"Patsy, you're gonna have to get him outta there." Deborah panted. "Take him back to the car before he freezes."

"Duck when you come aboard," Bridge muttered as Patsy approached the boat. His bloody finger waved in the air as he pointed toward the swaying boom. "Or that damn thing will knock you silly."

Patsy nodded, took a deep breath and stumbled onboard. The boat's filthy stench made her gag and the sloshing cockpit soaked her to the bone. She grabbed Charles and shoved him toward the side. "Come on, baby," she whispered. Charles' teeth chattered in response.

Charles crawled his way up onto the dock with Patsy pushing from behind. Once he was on the deck, Deborah let go of the rope and helped Patsy get Charles on his feet.

"Bridge, finish this," Deborah said. She cast a withering stare in Bridge's direction. "We're putting

Charles in the car before he catches his death."

Bridge took his time crawling onto the dock. "He's gonna be all right," he told himself. The image of the capsized boat behind the Normandie dissolved and faded from his thoughts. "A close call, but King Neptune lost this time." He looked back at his boat and a thin smile crossed his face. "Okay Chassy, that's your name."

Patsy held Charles close as she led him to the car. She felt his cold body shudder against her wet clothing.

"I'll start the car," Deborah said. "Get the heater going. He's freezing."

When the heater started running, Charles rested his head in Patsy's arms and fell asleep.

The champagne. After tying up the boat as best he could, Bridge staggered to Deborah's car and found the bottle of champagne in the back seat. He tapped on the driver's side window. "Come with me," he said to Deborah. "I need a witness."

There was no way to properly smash the champagne bottle against the bow like he'd seen done in the movies, so Bridge hurled the bottle toward the boat. The bottle shattered, spilling broken glass and champagne across the deck. The bubbly, yellow liquid dripped down the side into the water.

"Not very elegant, but I hereby christen thee the good ship Chassy." He gave Deborah a weary wink. "I'd say that's enough adventure for one day."

Deborah swept a lock of loose hair from her eyes with a muddy hand, leaving a brown smear across her forehead. She wiped her hands on her soiled dress, wheeled around and headed back to the car.

"One day my ass."

3

Two weeks after the accident, Bridge showed up at the Cicada Club fifteen minutes early for a fence-mending dinner he had arranged with his friends. An inviting atmosphere of spirited, yet muted sound and activity greeted him when the doorman, Francis, opened the door and gestured him in with a short bow. "Welcome back, Mister Appleton," Francis said.

Bridge nodded and gave his hat and coat to the coat-check girl.

Patsy promised to come and bring Charles, but Deborah never acknowledged the note he sent. To be safe, Bridge made the reservation at the end of Deborah's shift.

Bridge saw waiters setting up his table as he took a stool at the far end of the bar. "I'll have a scotch and soda," he said when Deborah approached him to take his order. He flashed an inviting smile while lighting a cigarette. "And add a dash of your trademark charm, will ya?"

Deborah nodded while she put down a napkin. She barely made eye contact and didn't reply.

Bridge's smile went stale after getting the cold shoulder. He knew not to bother Deborah while she was working and more than once she had cut him off with a flash of impatience, but this was serious. She had her hair tucked into a tight bun and wore a long apron over a no-nonsense skirt and blouse that did not appear to be chosen for a dinner engagement.

"Here ya are, Mister Appleton," the bar boy said, placing Bridge's tumbler over a napkin.

"Huh?" Startled, Bridge looked for Deborah. She had her back to him, working the other end of the bar.

Bridge always enjoyed watching Deborah

work. She never stopped; rinsing glasses, taking orders, mixing drinks, preparing ingredients and flirting with customers. She was a blur of movement. And usually Bridge was a focus in her activity. Tonight, though, sitting next to a chatty couple, Bridge felt invisible, alone in front of his drink.

"Mister Appleton?" Phillip, the club's Maître d'hôtel, came up behind Bridge's stool, ramrod straight in his starched collar and tails, clipboard in hand. "Your table's ready. Are your guests here?"

Bridge looked around the room. "I don't see 'em, Phillip. Hold it for another ten minutes, okay?"

"Ten minutes it is, sir." Phillip turned on his heel, put a finger in the air and signaled to somebody to hold the empty table. The four place settings of fine china, silver, and crystal gleamed under the soft lighting, waiting on an uninhabited island of fine linen and mahogany.

Out of the corner of his eye, Bridge saw Patsy hustle through the front door without stopping to check her coat. She was alone and didn't look happy. He waited for her to make her way through the crowd and pretended not to notice her.

"Oh Bridge, I'm so sorry." Patsy tapped on Bridge's shoulder. "But Charles has been battling a dreadful cold for days now." Bridge felt the cold night air lingering on Patsy's coat. "Excuse me," she said squeezing her way in between bar stools. The neighboring drinkers scooted sideways to make room.

Bridge turned his head and frowned at the sight as he waited for a peck on the cheek. Patsy's hair was undone, she wore no makeup and she was wearing an un-glamorous day dress and loafers.

"He insisted on coming," Patsy rattled on sounding like she had memorized the excuse. "But the moment I saw him I knew he was in no condition to make an appearance, especially here. Runny nose, watery eyes, coughing fits, fever, the works! I put him straight to bed."

Patsy caught Deborah's eye and waved as Deborah put away her apron. "I've missed you!"

"Likewise," Deborah handed her cash register keys to her replacement and held Patsy's hands over the bar.

"Goodness, what cold hands," Deborah said.

Patsy nodded, but didn't let go.

"I've been wanting to ask you," Deborah went on. "Did you ever find out who that guy was who towed the boys back? He looked so handsome standing on that big boat."

Patsy's eyes gleamed. "Remember the boat's name? Missy? It's Robert Taylor's boat all right. Said so in Photoplay Magazine. He keeps it at the Long Beach Yacht Club." Patsy raised an eyebrow and made a low whistle. "Swank place, I'm tellin' ya."

Deborah smiled, "Is that so. Well, what a coincidence, because my friend Emma saw him just last weekend at the Bullocks on Wilshire? She told me he was with some pretty young thing and they were looking at–"

Bridge cleared his throat loud enough to interrupt. "Can I interest you ladies in some dinner?"

"Sorry Bridge." Deborah pulled her hands free from Patsy's. "I have plans for this evening." She jutted her chin toward the relieving bartender. "Brendon will take care of your tab."

"Plans? I thought *we* had plans." Bridge nearly spilled his drink as he slammed the tumbler on the bar.

"Another time maybe." Deborah walked past Bridge, ignoring his plea.

"Let's finish this conversation later," she said,

pointing at Patsy.

"You betcha," Patsy said. She took a deep breath after Deborah left and looked back at Bridge. "Bridge, I hope you don't mind–"

"Would you care to eat at the bar, sir?" Phillip spoke up before Patsy could finish, his voice tinged with cold impertinence as he looked down his nose at the young lady.

Bridge looked at Patsy. "Care to join me?"

"Oh, I couldn't possibly." Patsy backed away and glared at the waiter as she turned to leave. A hint of pink rose up her cheeks. "Look at me," she said. "I'm not dressed for this joint. Let's make it another time."

"Just get me another scotch," Bridge said in the quiet after Patsy left. He stared at the ceiling and downed the remainder of his drink. "Make it a double."

Phillip raised his hand and the empty table was instantly filled with a party of four.

"Right you are, sir," Brendon said as he placed a freshly-filled tumbler on the bar. The amber liquid shimmered under the soft overhead lights.

That fall, when the sea breezes dissipated and the hot Santa Ana winds blew down from the inland deserts, Bridge gave up his sailing dreams.

"We're approaching the coast, sir. The outer buoys are in sight."

Two miles out to sea, and tacking into a brisk off-shore breeze, a beautiful fifty-two foot ocean racing yacht, Dorade, lowered its mizzen and foresails, reefed its main and made its final approach to Long Beach harbor under auxiliary power. It was on its return voyage from Hawaii having finished a record-breaking eleven-day crossing in the Los Angeles to Honolulu Trans-Pacific yacht race.

"Aye." A sturdy-looking man with a gruff beard looked landward from the forward cabin and studied the distant shoreline. Behind the city, the San Gabriel Mountains were covered with the season's first snowfall at the highest peaks. He acknowledged the news, ran his fingers through his mop of unruly hair, set his captain's hat firmly on his head and donned his blue blazer. "Raise the colors, Jameson, and clear the deck for arrival. Look sharp, now. Time to impress the moneyed class."

Among the yachting crowd, word was that nothing could touch the Dorade in any of the big, open-ocean races that year.

"She's in sight!" A lookout shouted from the Long Beach Yacht Club's upstairs reviewing room. The welcoming committee, assembled downstairs in the Club's trophy room, rushed outside. A man pointed toward a speck on the western horizon.

In the harbor, a fleet of boats, decked out with brightly-colored flags, set off for the harbor entrance. At the front of the fleet, Robert Taylor's 'Missy' sounded its horn.

The story of Dorade's string of successes had appeared in the sports and society pages. Yachting wasn't a big name sport on the west coast, but everybody loves a winner so the Long Beach Yacht Club, sensing a public relations opportunity, arranged to hold a gala victory celebration in honor of the Dorade's seven-man crew.

Back in the inner harbor, far away from the excitement, Chassy sat idle while King Neptune continued his tireless campaign to send the distressed craft to a watery grave.

Patsy's voice came as a surprise. Bridge wondered what was coming. He sat at his favorite desk in the family's oak-paneled library writing a letter to his aunt in Chicago when the phone rang.

"Bridge? Can we talk for a minute?" Patsy cooed over the telephone. "You still have that rusty old boat?"

"Chassy?" Bridge hesitated. He lit a cigarette to calm his nerves. "I haven't looked at her in a while. You want to buy her?"

"No, silly. I was hoping you still had it because it would be so much fun to take it to the Dorade party next month."

"The Dorade party? What's that?"

"Haven't you heard? The Dorade is a big yacht from Hawaii that won some kind of race. Everybody's talking about it. The Yacht Club's gonna throw a grand party and lots of dignitaries 'n movie stars will be there. But get this, we get in free if we show up by boat. Only your boat's gotta be cleaned up and nice looking, of course."

Bridge took a long drag on his cigarette. A fancy party full of big shots and glamour and high society. Maybe Deborah would like to go. But go in the Chassy? What a laugh. He blew out a long smoky breath and chuckled. That tub was practically consigned to Davy Jones' locker.

"Why don't I just get us all some tickets? My folks can get us in."

"What's the fun in that?" Patsy puffed. "All the swells will troop in the front door. Big deal. But we arrive by boat, all decked out and lookin' like a thousand bucks. We'll make a splash! Maybe even get our picture in the paper."

"Sorry, Patsy." Bridge thought about the accident and a chill ran up his spine. Charles gasping for breath, Deborah's anger, the capsized boat behind the

Normandie, his father's comment about King Neptune. "The boat's in no condition to go anywhere. If you're so fired up about going by boat maybe I can arrange to–"

"But Charles says he's willing to help fix it up." Patsy's voice got higher. "He's handy, you know, and he has some friends to help."

"Why are you interested in that boat all of a sudden? You know what happened."

"Because I think it's cute. You even said so. And, besides, I heard Robert Taylor is gonna be at the party. He's going in his boat and maybe he'd remember us."

"Aha." Bridge sighed. "So that's the rub."

Patsy paused for a moment and took a breath. "And when I asked Deborah, she didn't exactly say no."

Bridge sat up straight in his chair. "She what?"

"You heard me." Patsy stifled a giggle. "I think she'd come around if she knew we were having fun. We'll all pitch in. Whaddya say, sailor boy?"

Bridge twisted his cigarette butt in an ashtray and stared at the grey column of smoke. He wondered if he could make it up to her this way. Or would they all wind up dead? He had a vision of King Neptune sitting on his watery throne, laughing.

Bridge's mother walked into the room and rummaged through a stack of magazines.

"Sorry, Patsy." Bridge added finality to his voice. "But I don't think so."

"Will you at least think about it?" Patsy pleaded. "I know you're still upset about the accident and all. It just seemed like a fun way to get back together, like old times, you know? Promise me you'll think about it?"

"Sure. I'll think about it." Bridge looked at a framed photograph taken of him and Deborah in front of the Cicada Club right after it opened. Deborah's mother had taken the negative and had given them each a commemorative print, framed in silver. "I want you both to remember this day," she had said when she handed them the gift-wrapped packages.

That was five years ago. He remembered how happy he was. How radiant Deborah looked in the throng that celebrated the Club's opening night. He didn't want it to end this way; disappointed, defeated, alone. He had to try and mend the hurt feelings, but how?

"Thanks for calling." He softly replied, irritated by his mother's presence. "Say hi to Charles for me, will ya?"

"Sure thing, Bridge." Patsy let out a resigned sigh. "He says hi back."

"Who was that on the phone, dear?" Bridge's mother looked up from a magazine when Bridge hung up.

"Patsy."

"Patsy? You haven't mentioned her or her friend Charles in quite some time. They seemed like nice people. What's Patsy up to these days?"

"She wants to go on a boat ride."

Bridge's mother set down her magazine. "A boat ride? My goodness. I hope you're not thinking about doing something foolhardy."

"Of course not, Mother." Feeling uncomfortable with his mother's interrogation, Bridge lit another cigarette. "You heard me. I told her no."

"I also heard you say you'd think about it."

Bridge twisted around in his chair and forced himself to remain calm. "Don't badger me, Mother. I can think what I like."

"Of course you can, dear." Bridge's mother stood up with an exaggerated groan, one hand on her lower back. "I don't mean to interfere. I'm just concerned. There are other, safer ways to enjoy your friends' company."

"Please, Mother." Bridge frowned. "If you'll excuse me, I'd like to finish this letter to Aunt Dora and mail it before the post office closes."

After his mother left the room, Bridge scribbled a hasty end to his letter and decided to make a detour on his way to the post office.

Bridge found Patsy working the counter at the Foswell Corners diner on Wilshire Boulevard, a popular, unpretentious place to grab a quick lunch. Most of the customers were part of the blue-collar crowd that worked in the shops and businesses around Wilshire's so-called Miracle Mile.

She was busy handling the last of the lunch crowd, so Bridge stowed his hat and jacket on the crowded coat rack and took a stool at the counter. He watched Patsy work and thought about Deborah doing much the same thing. How come the women I know all work behind a bar?

"I'll have a ham on rye," he said when Patsy set a cup of coffee in front of him. "And hold the mayo."

Patsy pulled her pad from her apron pocket and a pencil from behind an ear. "One ham on rye, no mayo an' a cuppa joe." She leaned over the counter and winked. A strand of red hair followed the pencil and dangled down her neck. "Anything else, sweetheart?"

"Maybe I've changed my mind," Bridge whispered. He hesitated and looked at Patsy, concern on his face. "Can you promise Deborah'll come around?"

Patsy smiled, clipped the receipt to the order wheel and spun it toward the kitchen. "If you promise nobody falls in the drink."

Bridge lowered his eyes in resignation and lifted his cup off the counter with both hands. "I can't promise anything but the boat." He looked back up and frowned. "I guess I'm not the sailor I thought I was."

"Can I get some service down here?" A man down the counter raised and turned an empty cup upside down. A drop of brown liquid splashed on the counter.

"Keep yer shirt on, Kenny." Patsy turned away from Bridge to grab the steaming carafe off the coffee warmer.

"Patsy," Bridge raised his voice a notch to keep her attention. He pushed his coffee cup out of the way and leaned across the counter. "Tell you what. Tell Charles I'll come meet him at the dock Saturday morning, nine o'clock."

"Now yer talkin'," Patsy said. "Let's just see what happens."

A husky voice came through the kitchen pass-thru. "One ham on rye, up."

"Charlie Chan, my right-hand man!" Bridge gushed when he met Charles at the C dock gate. He put his hand out for a shake, then drew back when Charles didn't return the greeting.

"Howdy Bridge." Charles gave back a terse smile and pointed at his car. "I've brought company. Patsy told you about them, right?"

Two strangers got out of the car's back seat. They were dressed in overalls. One of the men spat a wad of chewing tobacco on the dock and blew his nose into an oily rag.

"This is Malcolm and Roscoe," Charles said gesturing toward the men. "They've offered to help resurrect that wreck of yours which once was a boat."

Bridge felt awkward from Charles' unfriendly greeting and the two scowling strangers added to his discomfort. "Howdy," he said and forced a smile as he raised his hand in their direction.

The two men waved their grimy hands, but said nothing in reply.

Charles pulled paint cans out of his car's trunk. "They're not volunteers," he said. "They'll cost ya five dollars apiece, per day. Plus materials."

Bridge nodded his agreement. "Fair enough, Charles." The chill in Charles' attitude smothered any chance for small talk.

"You been sailing any since... since the accident?" Charles kept his eyes forward while he and Bridge walked toward the end of the dock. Malcolm and Roscoe followed them carrying paint cans, brushes, and scrapers.

"No." Bridge shook his head. "I was planning on selling her. That is until Patsy called." Bridge took a deep breath. "I still plan to sell her after this shindig is over."

"Can't say that I blame ya," Charles replied. "It's too bad how things turned out."

At the end of the dock, the four men paused and stared at the little boat. It looked more abandoned than ever. A yellow stain on the boat's cabin marked the place where Bridge had christened it with champagne.

"Ain't nothin' a coat 'a paint can't improve," Charles said.

Roscoe made a low whistle. "In this case, maybe two or three."

Bridge cracked a wan smile and nodded at Roscoe in acknowledgement. "I hope you're right," he replied. He looked at Charles. "I heard you had a cold."

Charles turned to Malcolm and Roscoe. "This is where I nearly drowned."

The two men grunted. "Good a place as any," Malcolm muttered.

Charles chuckled. "Indeed. And all I got to show for it is this runny nose."

"Patsy said you and Deborah ain't getting along too well," Charles continued, looking at Bridge. "You really think fixing this boat is going to help matters?"

Bridge shrugged his shoulders. "You're right about me and Deborah." Embarrassed, Bridge shook his head. "I don't really know if this'll help anything. It's more Patsy's idea than mine."

"Last I heard, Deborah was pretty determined never to set foot on a boat, especially this boat. I hate for you to spend money and time on a lost cause."

Bridge nodded and looked down at Chassy. "It's a crazy plan. I know it. What got me interested is it's the first time Deborah and Mother have ever agreed on something. So it's got that going for it."

"Ha!" Charles laughed. "Well, Patsy sure likes the idea. I agreed to do this for Patsy's sake, so there ya go. Three against one. Maybe we can turn this sow's ear into a silk purse." He glanced at Bridge. "And have Prince Valiant win his Aleta in the bargain."

"One thing though." Charles' smile disappeared and he lit a cigarette. "No offense, but I'm not giving you get a second chance to kill me."

Malcolm and Roscoe stifled a laugh.

Bridge swallowed. "What do you mean?"

"Two things, actually." Charles pointed at the

ripped and soiled canvas that was still suspended in the rigging. "The only way I'll participate in this plan is we get rid of those."

Bridge looked at the sails then back at Charles. "But how will it move?"

"I got a better idea."

Bridge sighed. "And what might that be?"

"It has to do with an alternate propulsion system and that's all you need to know for now."

"Alternate what?" Bridge looked at Charles and furrowed his brow, waiting for more. He got a stony-faced glare back instead, so he decided not to press the issue. "OK, and the other thing?"

"I'm in charge of this shindig, as you call it." Charles stared at Bridge for a second, stony faced.

Bridge blinked and choked down a challenge to Charles' assertion. "That's fine with me, boss," he said instead, with a touch of sarcasm. He looked across the harbor and settled his hurt feelings. No sails, he thought. I can tell Mother I wasn't sailing.

Charles ignored the retort and spoke to his companions. "Now let's get this derelict out of the water and clean her up. Malcolm, put these paint cans on board. Roscoe, grab those brushes and scrapers and let's head over there."

Charles pointed toward a crane standing at the end of another dock. Small boats were sitting on wooden supports behind the crane.

"Those oars still on the boat?" Charles looked at Bridge.

Bridge nodded. "Last time I looked."

"Good. Now get on that leaky tub and help Malcolm paddle over to that crane. We'll meet you there."

At the end of the day, the Chassy sat high above

the dock atop a forest of pilings. Water dripped from a thick layer of green algae that hid the boat's bottom. The four men made a final walk-around, checking their work, and stopped in an open space. Sounds of hammering, scraping, and conversation came from other boats sitting on the pier.

"That's enough for today," Charles said. "Once it's dry we'll scrape, then paint."

Malcolm and Roscoe nodded but didn't move.

Charles looked at Bridge. "That'll be ten dollars, plus an additional three for the paint. Can you cover that?"

"It's kinda like a little tree house up there," Patsy said when she saw the boat sitting six feet above the dock. Curious about the refurbishing project, she begged Charles to let her see how the job was coming along.

"Don't get too close. The paint's still wet." Charles took off his hat and wiped his brow with a paint-spattered rag. He and Patsy stood in the boat's shadow. Empty paint cans littered the area around them along with a layer of dried paint chips and dead algae.

Malcolm and Roscoe were perched on ladders, painting one side of the boat's bottom with a new coat of blue paint.

"It looks swell!" Patsy waved at the painters. "You guys are doing a great job!"

The two men ignored her.

She squeezed Charles' hand. "Where's Bridge?"

Charles pursed his lips. "He said he'd help out, but he don't seem very enthusiastic. We haven't seen much of him since we got the boat out of the water."

"Huh," Patsy muttered. She stepped back into the sunlight, looked up and shaded her eyes with both hands. She cut a cute figure standing on her tiptoes, her red hair tousled by the sea breeze, and craning her neck to see over the boat's gunwale. "What color are you gonna paint the top part?"

"I'm thinking white. You got any ideas?"

"Red seems more fun, but I'm not sure. I think I'll ask Deborah."

Charles raised his eyebrows and gave Patsy a knowing smile. "Always thinking, ain't ya."

Patsy giggled. "If you can't get Bridge to help, I bet Deborah can."

Charles put his hat back on and tested the freshly painted hull with a finger. It was still tacky. He wiped his finger with a rag and pointed at his girlfriend. "You make this crazy plan of yours sound so easy."

4

"Good night, Francis." Deborah waved to the doorman and stepped out of the Cicada Club's front door into the cold night air. Once alone, she let go of her self-control and allowed the tears to come.

She took her time walking the half-block to her car parked on Melrose Avenue, hiding her face in front of shop window displays, thinking, brooding.

Seeing Charles staring back at her from the murky water haunted Deborah and there was nothing Bridge could say or do to change that. It was Bridge's fault. His brash, thoughtless bravado nearly cost Charles his life, yet Bridge acted like nothing happened. He wasn't even sorry. *A dash of trademark charm indeed. How dare he? I need to put an end to our relationship, once and for all.*

She all but yanked the door off her car. The Packard-8 rumbled to life and its motor sounds and smells of freshly-polished leather comforted her as she drove down Melrose toward home. She hid Charles' eyes in the traffic lights that glistened through the windshield.

"Patsy called," Deborah's mother said when Deborah arrived and found her in the kitchen wearing a flour-coated apron. She took one look at her daughter's red-rimmed eyes and hugged her.

Deborah gave her mother a peck on the cheek.

A loaf of bread sat on a rack above the stove, cooling. On the counter was a bowl with a cloth placed over it alongside a flour sifter, wooden spoons, and dribbles of dough. The warm kitchen was filled with the aroma of baking.

Deborah sat at the dining table, slipped off her work shoes and shook out her hair. Exhaustion and pent-up stress washed over her. She leaned on her elbows and propped her head up with both hands. With a heavy sigh, she shook her head and closed her eyes.

"Something the matter?" Deborah's mother put a flame under the tea kettle, cut two slices of bread and placed them on a plate with a knife and butter on the side.

Deborah nodded and sniffed.

The tea and warm, fresh bread opened the floodgates and a sob brought on another gush of tears.

"I can't keep it up anymore, Mama." Deborah took her mother's extended handkerchief and blew her nose. "I can't go on pretending I have any feelings toward Bridge. Not after what he did."

"You poor girl," Deborah's mother scooted her chair closer to her daughter's and patted Deborah's hand. "Have you two talked at all?" She broke off a piece of bread, buttered it and handed it to her daughter.

Deborah looked at the offering and shook her head.

"No. And I have no intention of doing so. He's so selfish and full of himself. Charles nearly died, Mama, and what does Bridge do? He invites everyone to a dinner party to 'mend fences.' I don't really care that he won't apologize to me, but he doesn't even try to reach out to Charles, or Patsy for that matter. Charles got a bad cold and I'm sure it's because he almost drowned."

Deborah's mother rolled her eyes and poured more tea. She thought for a moment before replying. "Bridge seems like such a nice young man." She added two teaspoons of sugar to Deborah's cup and stirred. "Maybe he's embarrassed to speak up. You know, ashamed, maybe."

Deborah pushed her chair away from the table. "If he's ashamed, he certainly doesn't show it." The two women looked at each other for a quiet moment, then Deborah dropped her eyes and stared at the floor. "He just doesn't care, Mama. And why should I?" She picked up her shoes and the slice of bread. "Thanks for the treat, Ma."

"Are you kidding?" Deborah balanced her telephone receiver in the crook of her neck while she put on her slippers. "I said I'd love to go to the Dorade party. I never said anything about going in Bridge's boat. I don't care how pretty it looks."

On the other end of the line, Patsy made a soft sigh. "I know how you feel, Deborah. Imagine how I feel."

Deborah gasped. "I know! You must be stricken sick. And that's what I mean. How could you even think about a boat ride?"

"Because this is about you, me, and Charles. I want us to get back together. The Dorade party would be so much fun. And Charles is doing a great job fixing that boat up. You could at least come and see it. Anyways, I need your advice."

"But I hate little boats, especially sailboats. *He* doesn't know how to sail and neither do the rest of us. Even fixed up, we'd never get to the party alive."

"It's not a sailboat anymore."

"What?"

"Charles borrowed something called an outboard motor from a friend of his. There won't be no sails."

"Outboard motor? What's that?"

"Charles says it's a little motor you attach at the back of a boat and it pushes the boat along, putt-putt-putt, like Robert Taylor's motorboat, only smaller, of course. Super idea, don't ya think?"

"Really? What about Bridge..." Deborah felt her throat tighten.

"Bridge maybe will go along for the ride, maybe not, I don't know. But Charles is in charge now. So nothing stupid will happen. We putt-putt to the party, have a great time and putt-putt back. Slick as a kitty's ear."

Deborah paused for a moment. "What did you mean about needing my advice?"

"The thing is, we can't agree on what color to paint the top part. I think red would stand out nice. Charles wants to paint it white. We thought you would have an idea. You're so good with colors–"

"Stop it, Patsy." Deborah let go with a thin smile. "You're such a conniver."

"C'mon," Patsy said with a giggle. "It's not even in the water anymore. Charles got it sitting on the dock like a little house. Only it's sitting on stilts. You gotta see it."

"Deborah's coming to see the boat on Saturday, just so's you know," Patsy said when Bridge picked up the phone.

Bridge's heart skipped a beat. "Really?" He looked around the den to make sure his mother wasn't there.

"You heard me. She's coming to see the boat, not you, of course."

"I understand." Bridge rummaged through his desk drawer for his pack of Viceroys. "Do you think she'll mind if I show up?" Behind Patsy's voice Bridge heard the sounds of dishes being scraped and food sizzling on a grill.

"I don't think so." Patsy paused for a moment and let out a long breath. "Long as you mind your p's and q's."

Bridge fished out a cigarette and struck a match. "I promise. What time?"

"In the morning. Around ten."

Bridge's mother came in the room. "Bridge, dear, have you seen my–"

Bridge cupped the phone's receiver, shook his head and gave his mother a sour look.

"Oh dear, I didn't know you were on the phone. Excuse me."

After his mother left the room, Bridge waited until the door was shut, then put the phone back to his ear.

"I gotta ring off. I'm at work," Patsy said.

Bridge took a drag off his cigarette and smiled. "Thanks," he said. "See ya there."

"Remember, be on your best behavior." A loud voice erupted in the background and Patsy hung up.

When he hung up his phone, Bridge gave a silent cheer. *I'll mind my p's and q's all right, and a lot more, besides.*

Bridge got out of his car when Deborah and Patsy drove up and parked next to Chassy's work site. Charles and his painters were putting the finishing touches to Chassy's bottom. The clear, sunny sky gave a hint of warmth despite a cool breeze that blew in from the ocean. Gone was the slimy coat of green algae that had covered the boat's planking and in its place, the bottom shone a bright blue that glistened in the afternoon sun. Up above the gunwale, the deck had been cleaned and sanded, and was waiting its turn.

He made eye-contact when Deborah got out of the car, but her icy stare cut off any chance for polite conversation. She looked as chic as ever, wearing a blue beret, navy blue sweater and a matching scarf along with white denim trousers.

"She's got enough blue paint on her to sink a battleship," Charles said as he climbed down a ladder to greet the ladies.

"Bad choice of words," Malcolm interjected and waved his paintbrush at Charles.

"Sink a what?" On the other side of the boat, Roscoe let out a mocking laugh.

"Hush!" Patsy hissed, glaring at Charles. "Don't you start sowing bad luck. Shame on you!"

"Sorry." Chastened, Charles hung his head and stood at the bottom of the ladder. "I meant she has enough blue paint to *float* a battleship."

Deborah laughed and waved. "Hi, Charles. It's a lot of paint, whichever way you look at it."

She purposely avoided looking at Bridge as she studied the boat with a serious look on her face. "Too bad most of that blue's gonna be under water. The top part needs to compliment the blue, but stand alone as well."

Walking behind the boat, Deborah's trouser legs paced the boat's perimeter, her boots' low heels clacking against the pier's wood surface.

"Pleased 'ta meet ya," Roscoe said as Deborah passed his ladder.

"Likewise, I'm sure," Deborah replied without stopping.

"A warm color like red or orange would stand out well," she said loud enough for everyone to hear.

Patsy poked at Charles and smiled.

"But they don't seem appropriate for a boat," Deborah continued. "A bold white with a different shade of blue trim, maybe a bit lighter, would seem nautical, don't you think?"

Charles poked Patsy back as Deborah came back around.

"Uh-huh," Bridge edged closer to the boat as Charles and Patsy nodded in agreement.

"There's a boat looks just like that over there," Malcolm pointed toward another sailboat, also on supports. "I been lookin' at it since we got started."

Deborah shaded her eyes from the afternoon glare. She studied the neighboring boat for a long minute.

"Kinda looks like you!" Bridge dared to say.

Deborah dropped her hand, turned around and for a moment, all was quiet.

Patsy put a finger to her mouth and bit down on a nail. "I think Bridge means the color. Not the boat, right?"

Bridge froze.

Deborah put her hands on her hips and gave

Bridge a stern look. "You may be a bridge, mister, but I most certainly am not a boat."

Roscoe failed to suppress a muffled guffaw from behind Chassy.

"Aw Geez, I didn't mean it *that* way..." Bridge stammered. He rubbed the back of his neck. "I just meant the colors were the same. You know? Blue and white?"

"Keep diggin' sailor," Patsy shook her head and sighed with relief.

Deborah walked back to Charles and Patsy, ignoring Bridge. "So that's my suggestion. White with a contrasting light blue trim. The boat name would look nice on the back as well, maybe in yellow or gold. Ya think?"

"Good idea," Charles turned to Patsy. "Could you make us a Chassy stencil?"

"Not sure how, but I'll try my best," Patsy replied.

"I can help with that." Bridge edged a few steps toward the group while Malcolm and Roscoe went back to painting.

Deborah crossed her arms and raised an eyebrow.

"Our next door neighbor owns a print shop in Van Nuys. Does stencils for the movie biz."

"You got the job." Charles pointed at Bridge. "It'll be your first step toward absolution."

Bridge's face lit up with satisfaction.

Patsy giggled.

Arms still crossed, Deborah kept a stony silence, but everyone noticed her eyes soften a bit.

A week later, when it came time to put Chassy back in the water, everyone cringed. The restoration project had put life back into the group's morale, but now, even as it glowed with its new paint and shiny fittings, the boat reminded everyone of its ominous past as it bobbed in the water. The Dorade party was the following Saturday.

"I'm having serious second thoughts about this whole thing," Deborah said. She paced back and forth on the pier and shoved her hands in her trouser pockets. Every time she looked down at the boat, she saw Charles' body bobbing in the water beside it.

Malcolm and Roscoe carried a long, rectangular wooden crate from the back of a borrowed pickup truck and sat it at the edge of the dock. Charles followed them with a red gas can. The smell of gasoline followed the men.

"Now before you go running for the hills, let me introduce you to the latest in watercraft propulsion technology," Charles said, as he assisted his two helpers in opening the crate with crowbars.

As the slats came off, shiny pieces of brass and steel appeared from under the packing material. One end consisted of a round container fitted with a protruding handle. Below that were some valves and hoses and a large vise. Two long metal tubes extended below the top and at the bottom of one tube, a propeller was attached.

"Is that the outboard motor you were telling me about?" Deborah stopped pacing and stood next to Patsy.

"Yup," Patsy replied. "Looks like something from Mars."

Deborah watched, wide-eyed, while Charles and his helpers lifted the motor out of the crate. As they moved it to the edge of the pier, Bridge and Roscoe climbed on board. Chassy and Roscoe followed.

"Be careful, it's heavy," Charles said as he and Malcolm inched the motor into Bridge and Roscoe's hands. Everyone held their breath as the heavy piece of equipment teetered above the water between the pier and the boat.

"I'll be damned," Bridge said as Roscoe tightened the motor's mounting vise and secured the motor snug against the boat's transom. "Looks like it was supposed to be there all the time."

"Don't mess up the paint!" Patsy hollered at the men. "It covers the boat name, darn it."

Deborah gave Patsy a sympathetic look. "You did great, Patsy. I can still see the name and the brass matches Chassy's lettering."

"Ta da!" Charles took off his hat and wiped his brow. He took Roscoe's place at Chassy's stern. "I'll give her some gas and we'll see what happens. Hank told me it should fire right up."

"Hank?" Bridge looked at Charles.

"Yup. He's a car mechanic. Works near my house. He got the outboard from a customer who needed a new transmission but didn't have any cash. Hank doesn't have a boat so he's letting me break it in. It's made by a company called Evinrude."

The strange attachment interrupted the clean lines of Chassy's hull, but it was small enough that it didn't seriously impair the boat's overall look. Still, it looked peculiar. When Charles closed the gas cap and adjusted the throttle control, Deborah moved back from the edge of the dock to get out of harm's way.

"It'll probably sputter some, first few tries," Charles said as he gave the start lanyard a slow pull to prime the throttle.

A plume of blue exhaust smoke rose from the motor's casing after the third try.

"C'mon baby," Charles said while the motor choked and sputtered. He twisted the throttle control handle back and forth.

Deborah took another step back.

"Cut back on the gas and hold 'er steady," Malcolm shouted over the engine noise. "Or you'll flood 'er."

Charles gave Malcolm a thumbs up. He turned the throttle control back a quarter turn and stopped adjusting.

The sputtering stopped and the exhaust cloud dissipated in the sea breeze as the motor caught and cycled smoothly.

Patsy clapped excitedly.

Deborah stood her ground, next to Malcolm, a concerned look on her face.

"Those little bitty motors don't need much gas to start," Malcolm gave Deborah a reassuring nod.

Despite not having any idea what Malcolm was talking about, Deborah nodded back in acknowledgement.

"Putt putt putt, just like I said," Patsy beamed.

Deborah and Malcolm moved a step closer to the action.

Charles put the motor in gear and, with a clunk, the water under Chassy's stern churned and swirled. The mooring lines stretched tight.

"Transmission works OK," Charles said. He shifted the motor back to neutral and decreased the gas. "I'm gonna let her warm up a bit."

"What's going on?" Bridge mumbled to himself under the noise of the outboard motor.

He stood in the boat's cabin passageway, looking at the scene around him. Charles was tinkering with the motor, Patsy was saying something to Charles from the dock, and Deborah was having a conversation with that painter, Malcolm, of all people. Nobody cared about him. Even though none of this would have happened if he hadn't bought Chassy in the first place.

It was a strange feeling, being ignored. Everyone was having a nice time without him.

Bridge moved out of the passageway and grasped the throttle control handle from behind Charles' back. The engine's vibration passed through his hand and arm. It felt strange and powerful. "So this makes it go?"

Charles bristled in surprise. He turned and faced Bridge, brow furrowed. "That's right. Twisting it to the right makes it go faster, to the left, slower."

"Sounds easy enough," Bridge gave the handle a slight twist to the right and the engine noise raised a notch. "Where's the brake?"

Charles smiled and nodded. "There's no brake like in a car, but reverse gear," he pointed to the gear shift lever under the engine's cowling, "kinda does the same thing." The letters D, N and R were inscribed on a grey metal plate behind the lever.

Bridge let go of the control handle and looked at Patsy and Deborah on the dock. The ladies stopped talking and stared back at him.

The hostility in Deborah's eyes made him hesitate. He took a gulp and made a big smile. "Why don't we take it for a test drive?"

"I don't think so," Deborah shot back.

A cloud passed overhead, covering the dock in shadow. Both ladies looked heavenward and shook their heads.

"Me neither," Patsy added. "It's been a long day

already."

Bridge hung his head, disappointed, and kept to himself.

Charles shut off the engine. The cowling's metal cover pinged as it cooled. "Hand me that cover, will ya?" he said to Roscoe who was standing next to the crate having a smoke.

"Thanks, Charles. It's been interesting." Deborah turned and walked toward her car.

"See ya tonight," Patsy waved at Charles. "Don't forget we're having dinner at your brother's place."

While Charles covered the engine, Malcolm and Roscoe smoked and waited. The ensuing quiet was deafening.

"I think the motor makes Patsy's crazy idea possible, doncha think?" Bridge forced a smile as he sat next to Charles and pulled out his wallet to pay the painters.

"That's what I'm thinkin'," Charles replied. The black canvas cover had 'Evinrude' stenciled on the front and back.

"I was also thinkin' we'd leave the motor on the boat for now," he added. "It's a lot of work, putting 'er on and takin' 'er off. Plus, I don't have anyplace to store it."

"Fine with me," Bridge nodded.

When Charles and the two painters left, Bridge stayed in Chassy's cockpit and lit a cigarette. The sun, low on the horizon, lit up windows on the east side of the harbor. A fishing boat chugged by, followed by a squawking flock of seagulls. He felt ignored and lonely, but Chassy's gentle rocking motion, generated by the fishing boat's wake, comforted him while he smoked.

The fishing boat blew its horn and Bridge saw his vision of the Normandie again, beckoning him. This time there were no sailboats in sight, Instead, a fleet of motorboats followed the ocean liner out to sea.

Maybe I've lost her, he thought while he studied the motor. Maybe it's over.

He stood up and removed the motor cover. The motor's parts still looked strange and he concentrated on the familiar pieces. He pointed and identified the parts he knew. "This is the throttle control handle, here's the starting lanyard, this must be the gear shifter..."

"I still got my boat, though." He twisted the throttle control to the right and pulled the lanyard.

The sudden noise and blue cloud of exhaust startled him, but he kept hold of the throttle control. The motor trembled in his hand and sputtered. "A little more gas," he recited over the noise. "Malcolm said not too much."

The motor settled into a smooth cycle and Bridge smiled with his accomplishment. The feeling of power pulsing at his fingertips thrilled him, replacing his despondent thoughts about Deborah with those of power and control.

"Ha! Nobody wants to take 'er for a test ride? It's my boat, dammit, I'll do it myself."

He held his breath, reached for the shifting lever, shoved it into the D position and quickly pulled his hand back.

There was a loud clunk and the motor labored, but nothing happened. Chassy stayed motionless at the dock.

What the hell?

Panic tightened Bridge's throat. He stared at the motor and then looked around the boat. Something was wrong, the boat wouldn't go, but he couldn't figure out... Wait a minute, what's this?

The mooring lines were stretched taut.

"You idiot." Embarrassed, Bridge looked up at the dock to make sure nobody was watching.

The lines were too tight to release, so Bridge moved the shift control back to N and the lines relaxed. The motor revved up and Bridge eased back on the throttle. He was still embarrassed, but felt good about handling the motor's controls.

After he released the lines, Chassy drifted away from the dock. An echo of panic ran through him, remembering the first time he left the dock, but Bridge concentrated on the purring motor. "We're partners," he said as he moved the shifting lever back to D.

This time, Chassy sprang to life and lurched forward toward the harbor's central channel.

"Shit!" Bridge lost his footing from the sudden movement and grabbed the motor's cowling to keep from falling. The hot metal burned his hand and he panicked, letting go of the cowling and dropping to his knees, his throbbing hand helpless, shaking in the air.

Out of control, Chassy turned in an arc and headed back toward the dock.

"How do you steer the Goddamn...?" Bridge held the throttle control arm with his other hand, hoping to reduce power, while trying to keep his balance in the pitching boat, he noticed the arm moved from side to side, causing Chassy to change direction.

"A-ha!" Forgetting about his injury, Bridge sat back down next to the motor and steered the boat away from the dock. The breeze, stirred up by Chassy's momentum, felt wonderful.

So this is how it's done.

While the last of the afternoon's light drained

into shadows, Bridge motored around the harbor, a big smile on his face.

5

"The cover's on backwards," Charles muttered. He'd come back to the pier the next day, alone, to pick up the last of the paint cans that had been left behind.

He stared at the outboard motor from the pier and scratched his head. The alteration stopped him in his tracks and he instinctively scanned his surroundings for intruders.

Nobody was in sight. "I know I put it on right." He stepped into Chassy's cockpit and looked for signs of tampering. The motor was turned to one side. He remembered leaving it sitting straight. The mooring lines were tied to the pier in disarray, not like he would handle them.

Charles repositioned the motor's cover correctly and re-tied the mooring lines. "Bridge," he said out loud.

Bridge initially said no when Patsy told him about Charles' plan for a rehearsal boat ride, but his triumphant motor cruise the day before made him change his mind. He felt liberated from Deborah's unforgiving attitude. All he wanted was a boat ride with his friends. The accident was terrible, and Deborah may never forgive him, but she couldn't deny him his ride.

Deborah, Patsy, and Charles waited next to him at the dock in stony silence. Nobody moved.

It was another crisp, fall day. Across the harbor, the Yacht Club was a hub of activity. Delivery trucks crowded the parking area and people were everywhere, stringing lights, setting up chairs, hanging banners. Tied to one side of the Club's harbor entrance, the Dorade sat in all her splendor. Pennants flew from both masts, and red, white and blue bunting was strung along her deck.

Charles had asked they have a rehearsal the day before the party. "Just a spin around the harbor is all," he said. "Get our feet wet, so to speak."

Bridge looked at the Yacht Club, then turned to face his companions. "Don't everybody talk at once," he said with a forced smile.

Patsy grabbed Charles' sleeve. "The plan is for Deborah and me to look beautiful while you swabbies take us to the Yacht Club. No funny business, right?"

"I can almost throw a rock over there." Charles squinted in the late morning sunlight. "Won't take us more than half an hour. We've got a spiffy little boat and a new outboard motor. What could possibly go wrong?"

Deborah let out a loud, bitter laugh that brought tears to her eyes. "That's great, Charles. That's just great. What could possibly go wrong? Well, let me count the ways."

Deborah's laugh rang bitter in Bridge's ears. He shook his head as her contemptuous tone drove home a sense of depression. Would it never end?

With a dismissive harrumph, Patsy climbed into the boat and took a seat. "Let's go." She looked at Deborah and scowled. "I know you're upset, Deborah, we all are, but your prima donna act is starting to wear me out."

Deborah's mouth dropped.

Patsy blew her nose and nervously fidgeted with her handkerchief. "You're my best friend, but I'm going to this party with or without you." A dash of color highlighted her cheeks. "You need to decide to either climb on board or go home. What's it gonna be?"

Deborah looked around the pier and back at the boat. Speechless, she shoved her hands in her trouser pockets and, head down, turned toward her car.

"Wait a minute." Bridge watched Deborah leave, then followed her. *Here's my chance, take it. What have I got to lose?*

"Don't leave," he said. "It's me you're mad at, not Patsy." He gestured back toward Patsy then looked at Deborah's distressed face. "It was my fault. The accident that is. "

Deborah slowed her pace.

Bridge took Deborah's hand. He hesitated. When she didn't resist, he held her hand with both of his. "I'm sorry for what I did." He turned to face Charles and Patsy. "I'm sorry for hurting all of you. I was a fool and my stupid pride nearly got Charles killed. All I wanted was for us to enjoy a boat ride. Please forgive me."

Deborah looked down at her shoes and took a deep breath. She held on to Bridge's hands.

Everyone waited.

Bridge cleared his throat. "I realize now I'm not–"

"Shut up, Bridge." Deborah looked into Bridge's face. Her eyes softened. "You're Bridge Appleton. Warts and all. I guess I just needed to hear you say that."

Deborah looked back at Patsy sitting in the cockpit. "Move over, sister, and let's get this show on the road."

As Bridge helped Deborah into the boat, she gulped and clutched his shoulder. Forcing a smile, she grimaced at Charles as she sat down. "I want to show up over there dry and in one piece. Nice and easy like.

No drowning, no drifting into breakwaters, and no wet feet!"

Charles nodded.

Bridge ducked into the cabin and handed out cushions. The calm morning warmed up with no wind.

He went back into the cabin. "Get comfortable, I'll be right back."

From inside the cabin, a cork popped.

"That's a nice sound," said Deborah.

Bridge came out of the cabin carrying a tray with a bottle of champagne and four stemmed glasses. "See how steady she sits?" he said. "Having you ladies on board makes the boat heavier and more stable."

"Not *that* much heavier," Patsy sniffed.

Deborah cracked a weak smile.

The bubbly champagne caught the sunlight as the glasses were passed around. And when the flutes were half empty, Bridge gave a mischievous smile. "How about it, Charles. Shall we start the engine?"

Charles looked at the ladies for permission.

Patsy grinned back and Deborah closed her eyes in submission.

Bridge had worried about the wind and swells on the night of the party but he needn't have. The dry, Santa Ana winds ended early that year and the onset of winter brought periods of cool, still nights.

Searchlights swept the skies in front of them when they parked Deborah's car at C dock. They could see colorful party lights strung along the breakwater. An intense glow emanated from the direction of the Yacht Club. Light radiated in all directions like rays from a second sunset.

The four of them watched the spectacle in silence for a moment.

"This oughta be a super party," Patsy said.

Everyone nodded and moved their belongings to the edge of the dock where Chassy sat waiting.

Bridge stood still. He scanned the black empty space in front of him and repeated in his mind the rehearsal trip they had taken the day before. Out past the green buoy to the mouth of the channel, then left past the lumber dock. Should be obvious from there. Took about half an hour, just like Charles said.

But now he couldn't see the buoy, much less the channel. Other than the distant lights there was no reference point. Visions of running into pilings and sinking in the middle of the channel ran through his head.

The ladies lit the cabin lantern and changed into their party dresses.

Charles came on board carrying a large sack that clanked when he dropped it into the cockpit.

"I don't think this'll work," Bridge whispered to Charles.

Charles smiled and pulled something out of the sack.

"I brought along some of these," Charles said and switched on a flashlight. The beam stretched across the water and illuminated the green buoy bobbing in the middle of the channel. "Figured they might come in handy."

"I'll say." Bridge gave out a sigh of relief. "Damn glad you did. Let's tie a couple to the top of the cabin and use 'em as headlights."

Patsy stuck her head out the hatch. "I got my dancing shoes and my best party dress on. Let's get this show on the road, boys."

Bridge and Charles caught a glimpse of Patsy's gown through the hatchway. It glowed pale yellow in the soft lamplight.

The outboard motor started up and purred after the first try and the boat moved quickly as Charles steered toward the shimmering glow of light.

When they passed the lumber dock, Bridge watched a procession of boat lights heading in the direction of the Yacht Club. He turned to Charles. "Shouldn't be hard to find our way from there."

"I hope they see us as well as we see them," Charles replied. He pulled out two more flashlights and switched them on.

Bridge stuck his head into the cabin. "Ladies, you ought to see this."

Boats of all sizes were everywhere, the larger ones were lit up and crowded. In front of them, the yacht club took up one entire side of the harbor. People were dancing and strolling. The familiar sound of Guy Lombardo and His Royal Canadians playing 'You're Driving Me Crazy' came across the water. The ballroom was an illuminated fairy castle.

While they all gaped, a horn blasted behind them. Bridge turned around to see a motorboat fast approaching. Bridge and Charles both pointed flashlights at the boat and hollered while Charles turned Chassy out of the way. The boat narrowly missed them.

"Hang on!" Bridge shouted.

The boat's wake was precipitous but not unexpected. Deborah and Patsy grabbed hand-holds as they climbed back into the cabin instead of panicking as Chassy rolled over the trailing swells.

In another minute, Bridge heard a second menacing sound coming from behind.

"Damn," he mumbled.

"More company comin'," Charles said.

The engine noise wasn't approaching as fast

as the last boat. In the blackness, Bridge and Charles pointed their flashlights at another hull, this one was much larger.

Suddenly, the outboard motor sputtered.

"That doesn't sound good," Patsy said, sticking her head out the cabin's hatch.

"Shine a light on the motor," Charles said as he crouched next to the throttle control.

One flashlight in each hand, Bridge shined a light on the approaching boat and another on the motor.

The motor died with a jerking thud. After three unsuccessful tries with the starter lanyard, Charles shook his head and stared at Bridge. "Out of gas," he said.

Bridge dropped the flashlights and cringed. His solo motorboat ride. *Oh, God. I used it all up.*

"That's strange." Bridge stared at Charles, mouth open in mock dismay. He raised his eyebrows trying to look concerned. "Why don't we have enough?"

A horn blasted behind them.

"What's goin' on out there?" Patsy's voice raised a notch. "Why've we stopped?"

Charles stood up and wiped his hands. "You tell me, Bridge. Everyone saw me fill it up when we started." He took a step towards Bridge, hands clenched. "There ain't no leak. Should'a been enough."

Bridge ran his hands through his hair and avoided Charles' stare.

He sat down and took a deep breath. "OK. It's my fault... again." Bridge whimpered. "I took her for a spin that day you installed the motor. I wasn't gone long, an hour tops. Didn't think it'd make any difference, ya know?" He gave Charles a pleading look.

His voice trailed off as he sat down, put his hands over his face and shook his head. "What are we gonna do?"

Another motorboat roared by, rocking the boat. Then another horn from behind. Longer this time. The cabin remained silent.

"We still have those oars?" Charles said.

Bridge dropped his hands, looked at Charles and gritted his teeth, half in relief and half in anxiety, not sure if the oars were still on board. "Yeah, the oars. Let me look."

A spotlight illuminated Chassy from high above them. The intense cone of light stopped Bridge in his tracks.

A man's silhouette stood at the boat's bow. Then a voice boomed, "Could you use a hand there?"

Charles waved his hat. "I recognize that voice! You saved us from the breakwater!"

The figure roared back a laugh. "I remember you as well. Going to the club?"

Music and laughter came through the boat's lit-up portholes.

"Darn tootin' we are!" Patsy climbed out of the cabin and shouted back. "Soon's we navigate through all these yahoos around us!"

More laughter emerged from the big boat.

Deborah clung to Patsy's shoulder and followed her out.

The man disappeared and the boat's motors dropped to a gurgling, deep-throated rumble.

"Please accept my invitation to join our landing party," the silhouette returned.

"By gosh, I was right. It *is* Robert Taylor!" Patsy whispered. Both girls' eyes widened.

Deborah turned toward Bridge, grabbed his hand and smiled at him for the first time in a long while. "Keep talkin' sailor."

A surge of warmth filled Bridge's chest. He smiled into the light and shouted at the silhouette. "Don't mind if we do."

A line dropped into the cockpit. Another line fell at Chassy's bow.

"Secure your boat with our lines and we'll send down a ladder. I promise not to pitch you overboard this time."

As the rope-ladder made its way down, the spotlight focused on Deborah standing at Bridge's side. Rhinestones, sequins and shimmering gold brocade reflected the light into a glowing pool of color and sparkle, revealing a stunning female figure who teetered in Chassy's rocking cockpit.

From somewhere above them, a wolf whistle pierced the night air.

"Easy does it, girl." Bridge summoned his courage and gingerly put his arm around Deborah's waist to steady her as the big boat closed in.

Deborah took his hand and held tight.

Someone yelled, "Hey lovebirds, turn this way," and somewhere a flashbulb popped.

Bridge shifted his fedora to cover their faces and whispered close to Deborah's ear. "See ya in the movies, doll."

Jim White can't spell, he has a hard time keeping names and places straight and organization is a challenge for him. But he loves to write and can tell a good story. After thirty years writing for the wrong reasons, he said good bye to a technical writing career in Silicon Valley and started writing for himself. He's never turned back.

He discovered he had a lot to write about; a master's in American History, a Viet Nam veteran, a high school teacher, technical writer, librarian, laborer, sailor, proud father and devoted husband. He also came from a family of letter writers and their trove of letters about world events and every day trivia since the 1920's is an important cache of inspiration.

The result has been a string of publishing successes; a non-fiction publication, 'Great Expectations, the business correspondence of Gibbons & Lammot gold rush black powder merchants,' was published by the California Historical Quarterly. Fiction short story and novella publications include, 'Unified Field,' Chronoscope Magazine, 'Cisco,' scheduled for publication by Dark Passages Publishing in Fall, 2017, and 'Vistula,' a story about the siege of Warsaw during World War II from the perspective of a Polish-American GI who deserted his post and joined up with the Polish Resistance forces in 1944, in Storylandia, Issue 28, Autumn 2018. More about Jim White can be found at www.myjotting.com.

Thank you to the Wapshott Press sponsors, supporters, and Friends of the Wapshott Press.

Muna Deriane

Kathleen Warner

Rachel Livingston

James and Rebecca White

Jennifer Bentson

Debbie Jones

Steven Acker

Ann Siemens

Suzanne Siegel

Aubrey Hicks

Carol Colin

Ted Waltz

Kathleen Bonagofsky

Cynthia Henderson

Nancy Lilly

Jeff Morawetz

Patricia Nerad

Amanda Nerad

Elaine Padilla

Laurel Sutton

Deana Swart

The Wapshott Press is a 501(c)(3) not-for-profit enterprise publishing work by emerging and established authors and artists. We publish books that should be published. We are very grateful to the people who believe in our plans and goals, as well as our hopes and dreams. Our new website is at www. WapshottPress.org